NINTENDO® HEROES

Link and the Portal of Doom

Logan Lake Literacy
loganlakeliteracy@gmail.com

NINTENDO HEROES®

Link and the Portal of Doom

By Tracey West

SCHOLASTIC INC.

New York   Toronto   London   Auckland   Sydney
Mexico City   New Delhi   Hong Kong   Buenos Aires

No part of this work may be reproduced in whole or in part, stored in a retrieval
system, or transmitted in any form or by any means, electronic, mechanical,
photocopying, recording, or otherwise, without written permission of the publisher.
For information regarding permission, write to Scholastic Inc., Attention: Permissions
Department, 557 Broadway, New York, NY 10012.

ISBN 0-439-84364-2

TM & © 2006 Nintendo. All Rights Reserved.

Published by Scholastic Inc.
SCHOLASTIC and associated logos are trademarks and/or
registered trademarks of Scholastic Inc.

12 11 10 9 8 7 6 5 4 3 2 1   6 7 8 9 10/0

Printed in the U.S.A.
First printing, May 2006
Designed by Neo9 Design Inc.

Cucco Trouble

"Help! Help!"

Link's pointy ears twitched as he heard the cry. He paused. He was journeying on the outskirts of Kakariko Village, the small settlement just outside the majestic towers of Hyrule Castle. He couldn't tell if the sound was coming from the trees up ahead or the farmhouse farther to the right.

Navi, the tiny, shimmering fairy who acted as Link's guide, glowed a soft green.

"Someone is in trouble at the farm," Navi informed him.

Link nodded and ran toward the farm-house. Ever since he had agreed to help Princess Zelda cast out the evil that threatened Hyrule, every cry for help sent Link's heart pounding. Had the dark figure that threatened him in his nightmares finally come to life? Link sprinted swiftly across the grassy field.

The cry came from a distraught-looking farmer, a skinny man dressed in well-worn overalls. He stood in front of a rickety pen made of spindly logs.

"Are you in danger?" Link asked him.

"It's my cuccos!" the farmer wailed. "They've all disappeared!"

Link sighed. It seemed like none of the villagers could keep track of those brainless birds.

"They've probably just wandered off," Link told him.

But the farmer shook his head. "Not my cuccos! Something terrible has happened. I can feel it." He glanced into the woods behind the farm. "I bet it's wolves."

Link looked toward the trees. The farmer could be right. And if wolves were threatening the village, it was his duty to find out.

Link patted the sword at his side. "I'll help you," he said.

A look of relief replaced the worry on the farmer's face. "Thank you," he said. "Be careful out there, boy."

Link turned without saying a word. *Be careful, boy.* Ha! If that farmer knew what Link had seen, what he had fought already, he wouldn't tell him to be careful.

Link could handle anything that crossed his path.

Navi fluttered ahead as Link silently entered the woods surrounding Kakariko Village. Even though he was just looking for some confused cuccos, it paid to be cautious. You never knew what was hiding in the woods these days.

Cluck cluck CLUCK!

Something whizzed past Link's cheek. He jumped, startled. A mass of white feathers zoomed through the trees.

A cucco? It couldn't be. Cuccos could barely get off the ground, much less fly at lightning speed. But that was what it had looked like. Link charged after it.

Running as fast as he could, Link almost caught up to the bird. It was a cucco all right, but it wasn't flying. It was as though some unseen force was pulling it through the air.

As Link ran, the trees thinned out a bit and a stone wall came into sight. Link cringed. The cucco was sure to smash into it.

Instead, the wall sucked the bird right inside it! Surprised, Link slowed his pace. The cucco had vanished into a swirling vortex of dark wind.

"Link, be careful!" Navi warned in his ear.

But the warning came too late. Link felt a magnetic pull grip his body.

He was being sucked into the vortex!

A Mysterious Map

Link dug his heels into the dirt, but the vortex at the center of the wall pulled him closer. As he reached the wall, an otherworldly coldness touched his skin.

With all his strength, Link grabbed the top of the wall. The vortex sucked at his body, pulling the cloth of his green tunic closer and closer to the swirling winds. Link fought the pull, heaving himself to one side. The pull released him as soon as he was no longer directly in front of the vortex.

"It's some kind of portal," Navi said, emerging from a safe spot behind Link's head.

"If it's a portal, then it must lead somewhere," Link remarked.

Navi blinked thoughtfully. Link's fairy guide knew just about every inch of Hyrule.

"It is unnatural," she said finally. "It seems to lead to some other dimension."

Link remembered the strange chill he had felt. "Probably not a nice one," he said. For a second, he felt sorry for the cuccos. "This thing's a menace. Isn't there some way to close it? Some kind of door or something?"

"Look closer," Navi instructed.

Link stepped back from the wall. An inscription had been carved into it

7

underneath where Link's hands had just rested. Below the words was what looked like a map of Hyrule.

"It's ancient Hylian," Link said. "I can't read it."

He frowned. Maybe the map would be more useful. As he examined it more closely, Link noticed that five musical notes, each marked with a different number, dotted the map. It was interesting, but it didn't show him how to close the portal.

"*Hoot! Hoot!*"

The sound jolted Link from his thoughts. He looked up to see a large brown owl perched on a tree branch overhanging the wall.

Link smiled. "Kaepora Gaebora," he said. "Have you come to help?"

"If you like," the owl replied. "I can read ancient Hylian."

"I appreciate your help," Link said.

Kaepora Gaebora read the words inscribed on the wall:

"Open I will, when the stars align
and the full moon hangs in the
*   summer sky.*
A door to a world beyond this world.
A world of danger, terror, strife.
Close I will, when the song is played.
Close till the stars align once more."

Link frowned. Navi was right — the portal led to another dimension, and from the inscription, it didn't sound like a good place to visit. Link thought of the inscription's words again. Somehow astral convergence must have opened the portal. And the only way to close it was with a song? *What song?* Link wondered.

Link's eyes strayed to the map. The five musical notes seemed to leap out at him.

"The map is the key," Link said. "It leads to the song. There must be five parts to it — one part for each musical note on the map."

Link took a rolled-up piece of parchment from inside the pack he carried with him. He searched the ground until he found a piece of soft, black rock. Then he placed the parchment over the map and began to rub with the rock. An imprint of the map began to appear.

Kaepora Gaebora nodded approvingly. "Very smart," the owl said.

Link tucked the map inside his pack. He had pledged to help Princess Zelda save Hyrule. This portal was definitely a threat to the land. He knew it wouldn't be long before the vortex started sucking in more than a few stray cuccos. If the only way to close it was with a song, then Link would just have to find that song.

Link looked up at the owl. "Thank you," he said.

"You're welcome," replied Kaepora Gaebora. "Just call me if you need me."

Link marched back through the woods.

"Where are we going?" Navi asked, fluttering around his face.

"We're going to find a song," Link replied. "The first musical note on the map is in Hyrule Field. We may as well start there."

Navi blinked in agreement, and the two continued on. Hyrule Field was a large stretch of land that took almost a day to cross. However, the musical note on the map appeared in the eastern portion of the field, and Link knew it wouldn't take too long to get there.

Link and Navi quickly reached the field from Kakariko Village. While they walked through the field, the orange sun began sinking into the horizon. Navi's wings began to beat quickly against Link's cheek.

"It will be dark soon," she said nervously. "We must be careful!"

"Rats!" Link muttered. He should have known better. Hyrule Field was a safe place during the day, but dangerous creatures came out in the dark of night. Link had lost track of time while trying to figure out how to close the portal. But it was too late to turn back now.

The darkness seemed to be falling more quickly now, as though someone were speeding up time.

"We just need to get on the path," Link
said. "We'll be —"

Something grabbed Link's ankle, and
he fell flat on his back. A skeleton hand
had burst from the dirt, and now it gripped
him with an unnatural force.

"A Stalchild!" Link cried.

A Message from Zelda

The ground rumbled as three pairs of skeletal hands burst through the crumbling earth. Link kicked violently, freeing his ankle from the monster's grasp. He jumped to his feet and drew his Deku Sword and Deku Shield.

The skeletons pushed all the way out of the ground now, fixing their dark, hollow, eyes on Link. In his travels, Link had faced monsters far more dangerous, but the dead-eyed Stalchilds always chilled his blood.

Link lunged at the Stalchilds with a

series of quick cuts, but they had him surrounded now. Link moved swiftly, slicing his sword as he turned.

Smack! His sword connected with one of the Stalchilds. The creature tumbled back and then ran off into the darkness.

They look awful, but they're not as brave as you'd think, Link reminded himself. He turned to face the other two monsters.

Slash! Another Stalchild reached out and clawed Link with a bony hand, slicing his green tunic and scratching his arm. Angry, Link struck back. The Stalchild crumbled at his feet.

Without stopping, Link swung his sword around, striking the last Stalchild in the rib cage. The blow sent the creature flying backward.

Link nodded, satisfied. But without

warning, the Stalchild at his feet gripped both of his ankles. Link struck with another blow from his sword, and the Stalchild let go. But the momentum sent Link falling backward.

Whack! Link's head smacked against a rock sticking out of the dirt. His breath left him in a harsh gasp, and then everything went dark. . . .

Link felt his body swirling, whirling, as though he were trapped in the vortex again. Dark clouds surrounded him, and his body felt cold.

And then, suddenly, the darkness parted, and Link saw the face of Princess Zelda in front of him. There was concern in her large blue eyes.

"Wake up, Link," she said. *"Help is just beyond the oak trees. Wake up."*

"Wake up, Link! Wake up!"

Link opened his eyes and groaned. He sat up, rubbing the bump on the back of his head. Navi anxiously fluttered around his face.

"Are you all right?" she asked.

"I think so," Link replied. He still felt groggy. Then, suddenly, the memory of his recent battle came to him.

"The Stalchilds!" he cried. He tried to jump up, but he was unsteady on his feet.

"You took care of them, Link," Navi said. "But I'm worried. I think you need help."

Help is just beyond the oak trees. Had he really seen Princess Zelda? Or was it some kind of dream? He scanned the trees on the edge of the field.

Just off the path, two large oak trees formed an archway with their branches. Link walked toward them.

🏹 🏹 🏹 🏹 🏹 🏹 🏹

"Where are we going?" Navi asked, but Link didn't answer. He wanted to be sure.

A large, round boulder sat just past the trees. It was an odd place for a boulder, Link knew. And that usually meant one thing.

Link took a small blue bomb from his pack. He lit the fuse with his Deku Torch and hurled the bomb at the boulder.

"Run!" Link cried. Navi flew behind him as he darted away.

BAM! The bomb exploded, blasting the boulder to sand. When the smoke cleared, Link walked up to where the boulder had stood.

It was just as he had thought. The boulder had blocked a passage to an underground grotto. Link and Navi climbed down into a dark tunnel.

The tunnel opened into a chamber filled with soft, glowing light. Water bubbled in a stone fountain at the back of the chamber. The glow came from five tiny fairies who darted among the flashing drops. They blinked with excitement when Link entered.

"You are hurt," one of them said.

"We can help you," said another.

The fairies began to glow brighter. The white light washed over Link, and instantly the pain in his head was gone. He felt lighter, stronger, as though he had just had a full night's sleep.

"Thank you," Link said. "Princess Zelda said you would help me."

The fairies blinked in response. Link turned to leave the grotto, but something made him stop.

The fairies sang a simple tune . . . just five notes, but they kept repeating them.

Excited, Link took out his map. The musical note on the Hyrule Field was just about where the grotto was located. Could this be the first part of the song?

Into the Lost Woods

Link took out the Fairy Ocarina given to him by Saria, his friend from Kokiri Forest. He put the small flute to his lips and played the notes along with the fairies.

The fairies blinked in different colors to show their happiness. Link put away the Fairy Ocarina and took out his map. He was surprised to see that the first musical note on the map was glowing.

"I think you found the first part of the song!" Navi chirped in his ear.

"I think so, too," Link said. He put the ocarina and map back in his pack. "Thank you so much. You have helped me more than you know," Link said to the fairies.

Link and Navi emerged from the grotto and found that morning had dawned. Time had a funny way of passing when you were around fairies. Then again, he had no idea how long he had been unconscious. Link and Navi had to move fast. They were losing valuable time.

"The second part of the tune is in the Lost Woods," Link said. "We had better move fast."

When Link reached Kokiri Forest, his home, the forest's elflike inhabitants were just waking, leaving their homes to greet the early morning sunlight. Link nodded as he passed. There was no time to talk today. He was on a mission.

The green leafy woods became darker and more crowded, and when they reached the Lost Woods, Link knew he had to be careful.

He had always thought Kokiri Forest was a beautiful place, where sunlight reached down through the trees to coat everything in a warm glow. But today the sun seemed to have overlooked the Lost Woods. Now the trees were a complicated maze of twists and turns. Link took out the map and studied it. The musical note was located in a small glade in the center of the woods. Link planned out his route, then put away the map.

Link marched through the woods, staying on the path until he came to a crossroads. He made a right turn, knowing it would lead him to the center.

"You seem to know exactly where you're

going," Navi remarked. "You don't need me to guide you."

"I always need you, Navi," Link said, smiling. Every Kokiri child received a fairy guide when they were young. Link had waited longer than usual for his, and he was happy to have her.

They walked on, and Link made another turn. He replayed the tune of the fairies in his head. He didn't want to forget it!

Thunk! The loud sound broke his train of thought.

Thunk! Something whizzed past Link's ear, and he spun around. Two Deku Scrubs ran toward them. The small brown creatures had leafy tops and long snouts that enabled them to shoot Deku Nuts at passersby. Link frowned. They must have strayed from their home in the Deku Tree.

Link quickly raised his Deku Shield. *Thunk! Thunk! Thunk!* The nuts harmlessly bounced off.

Link jogged backward, hoping to outrun the scrubs. They wouldn't give chase for long, he knew, and he didn't feel like engaging in another battle. He darted around the corner and then ran until he was sure the Deku Scrubs were far behind.

When Link finally stopped, he looked around him. The path led in two directions. But which should he take? His encounter with the Deku Scrubs had confused him.

"Maybe I can help after all," Navi said. She flew toward the right path. "Listen."

Link followed Navi. In the distance, he could hear a faint noise, like the sound of birds.

Link jogged toward the sound. It had to be the second part of the song! He turned a corner, and the sound grew louder. . . .

"Link! Look out!"

Link stopped just as a Skutulla dropped down in front of his face. The creature looked like a giant spider with an image of a skull on its back. Its six red eyes glowed menacingly, and a foul-smelling liquid dripped from its sharp fangs.

Link quickly ducked. It was no use attacking a Skutulla head-on; its armored body was nearly impossible to pierce. Link somersaulted, landing on his feet just behind the Skutulla. He knew its soft underbelly was the only place it was vulnerable. Link quickly speared the creature. Now the Skutulla hung limply from its thread.

"Nasty business," Link said, shaking his head and remembering the birds' song. "Thanks for the warning, Navi."

Navi blinked. "I think the birds are this way, Link."

Link followed Navi, and the growing sound of the birds led them to a tree in the middle of a small glade. Five birds sat on a branch, happily chirping the same five notes over and over again.

Link checked the map. Sure enough, the second musical note began to glow. Link took out his ocarina and joined in. The birds flapped their wings, pleased with the accompaniment.

Suddenly, the birds took flight. They flew in a circle around Link's head. Then they flew out of the glade, as if beckoning Link to follow.

Link chased after them. They finally perched on a bush near a tunnel that had been carved into the bottom of a hillside.

"It's some kind of shortcut," Navi told Link. "They're trying to help."

Link nodded to the birds. "Thank you," he told them.

Then he and Navi walked inside the tunnel.

5

The Road to Death Mountain

Link lit a Deku Stick to light their way as they traveled through the tunnel. To his relief, the dark passageway held no nasty surprises. When they finally emerged, Link found himself standing in front of the marketplace.

"That's strange," Link remarked. "Goron City, the next spot on the map, sits high atop Death Mountain. Why did the birds lead us here?"

"Maybe there is something here you will need," Navi suggested.

Link felt the right pocket of his tunic. It held about one hundred rupees — all earned from helping others along in his past journeys. He scanned the crowded marketplace, which contained stalls that sold anything one could imagine. The glistening glass bottles at the front of the potion stall caught his eye.

A healing potion would have come in handy earlier, when he had banged his head. Link approached the stall and purchased a green potion for thirty rupees, the going rate. He tucked it into his pack. His stomach was rumbling, so he spent a few more rupees on some bread and cheese. He wolfed down half of it, then put the rest in his pack to eat later in the journey.

When he was done, he turned toward a tall mountain which rose in the distance, just past Hyrule Castle. It was Death

Mountain. The mountain was home to many dangers, including rolling boulders and strange creatures, but it was also home to the peaceful Gorons. It was there he would find the next part of the song.

Link started to leave the marketplace, but something caught his eye in one of the stalls. Curious, he moved closer.

Amid a display of arrows and slingshots hung a shiny silver shield with red and yellow markings on the front. Link had seen the Hylian Shield before, but his pocket had been empty of rupees then. He looked down at his Deku Shield, which had served him well, and which would surely serve him again. But the wooden shield wasn't able to protect him from all dangers. The Hylian Shield could come in handy. . . .

"Eighty rupees!"

The stallkeeper, a tall, muscular man with a long black mustache, barked the price in Link's face. Link looked at the coins in his hand. He had seventy rupees left.

"Sixty," Link offered.

"No good," said the stallkeeper. "Seventy-five."

Link hesitated for a moment. Did he really want to spend all of his rupees? But the shield was practically mesmerizing him. . . .

"Seventy," Link said firmly.

The man nodded. "The shield is yours. It's a fine piece, forged from the fires of Hyrule's finest blacksmith."

The stallkeeper took the shield down from the wall and handed it to Link, who accepted it breathlessly. The shield felt hefty in his hand, and holding it made him feel like a real warrior.

Link looked at Navi. "I think I'm ready for Death Mountain now."

It took nearly all afternoon for Link and Navi to walk to the foot of Death Mountain. As Link climbed the steep slope leading up to Goron City, he kept an eye out for hidden dangers. By the time he reached the entrance to the great cave that led to the city, the sun was setting once again.

Link stepped into the cave and let his eyes adjust to the darkness. Bomb Flowers grew along the cave walls, and a torch hung next to the opening. Link used a Deku Stick to light the torch. Then he took out the map.

"The spot on the map is not far from here," Link said. "This should be easy."

Link put the map back in his pack. When he looked up, he saw two large red eyes coming toward him from the darkness of the cave. Link held the torch in front of him. Two hideous four-legged creatures crawled toward him.

"Tektites!" Link cried.

Gorons' Rock!

Link thought quickly. One bite from a Tektite could cause excruciating pain — or worse. He didn't want to get close enough for swordplay.

Link leaned the torch against the cave wall and drew his Fairy Bow and Arrows. He strung an arrow in the bow, took aim, and then let it fly.

Zing! The arrow hit its mark. The creature squealed and skittered away.

Angered, the other Tektite charged toward Link. Keeping a steady hand, Link strung another arrow. The Tektite came closer, closer. . . .

Zing! The arrow hit its mark again, and the Tektite crumpled to the floor of the cave. Link picked up the torch, cautiously stepped over the fallen creature, and then ran ahead into the cave.

He and Navi hadn't gone far when the cave split into three passageways. Link took out the map and determined the center path was the way to go. He walked on . . . only to find the tunnel ahead blocked by a boulder.

"Rats," Link muttered. He looked at the map again. He clearly needed to continue on this path, but he had used his last bomb in Hyrule Field. He moved the torch back and forth, searching for another way. But all the flames illuminated was a cluster of Bomb Flowers. . . .

"Of course!" Link said. Normally, Bomb Flowers were too heavy for anyone but Gorons to pluck. Luckily, the leader of the Gorons had given Link a special bracelet that would give him all the strength he needed.

Link bent down and plucked one of the heavy blooms. The boulder wasn't huge; one flower should do it. Link took several steps back.

"Get behind me, Navi," he said. He lifted his shield, then tossed the bomb at the boulder.

Bam! The boulder exploded into pieces. When the dust cleared, Link lowered his shield.

Glowing torches lit the pathway ahead. Link stepped through the hole and headed down the path. Soon the unmistakable sound of music reached his ears.

Link turned the corner to find himself in a small chamber. Glimmering crystal stalactites descended from the ceiling. A Goron stood in front of them, holding a wooden mallet.

The sight of the Gorons always intrigued Link. They were large people, with round, yellowish bodies that looked like they had been carved from stone. Their heads were smooth and pointy, and most Gorons had rocky ridges going down their back. Their large, dark eyes revealed their kindness.

This Goron smiled when he saw Link.

"Do you like my music?" he asked. "I am practicing to play at a big feast tonight."

Link smiled, imagining a Goron feast. Gorons loved to eat one thing — rocks!

"I do like your music," Link said. "May I hear it again?"

"Sure," said the Goron. He began to hit the crystals with the mallet, playing five notes over and over again.

Link looked at the map, and the third musical note began to glow. It was the third part of the song! Link took out the Fairy Ocarina and joined in. He played the tune over and over until he had memorized it.

The Goron was pleased. "You must come to the feast! You make good music! You will be our guest."

Link was about to say no, when he realized how tired he was. He was not sure how long it had been since he had slept. If he grew too tired, his reflexes would be slow, and that was dangerous. After all, he had to rest sometime.

"It would be my honor to be your guest," Link said.

Link spent the night listening to Goron music and enjoying their hospitality. Afterward, he fell into a deep sleep and arose hours later. Thanking the Gorons, Link and Navi left the cave and stepped back out onto Death Mountain. The rising sun streaked the sky with shades of orange and gold.

"Good. It's early," Link said. The map showed that the fourth part of the song was located in Dodongo's Cavern. Even though Link had defeated the Dodongos, the dinosaurlike people who inhabited the cave, it would still be better to go there in the daytime. The cavern was now much safer, but memories of the Dodongos still made him shudder.

After a long trek, Link and Navi found the entrance to the cavern and stepped inside the first chamber. According to the map, the song was located just two chambers away. If all was clear, he should have the fourth part of the song in no time.

Link crossed the first chamber and found a ladder that led up to the next level. When he reached the top, a green snout stared down at him. For a second, Link froze with fear. He was face-to-face with a Lizalfos!

Hissssssssss! The Lizalfos stuck out its long red tongue. Startled, Link fell backward through the air. He landed back on the chamber floor with a thud. Before he could get to his feet, the Lizalfos jumped down on top of him!

Danger in Dodongo's Cavern

Link rolled away as quickly as he could, but the Lizalfos was faster. *Slash!* The reptilian creature managed to strike Link's leg with his sword.

Link winced in pain and rolled away. He had fought Lizalfos before, and knew that these creatures were impossible to defeat unless you could slow them down. A Deku Nut usually did the trick, but he had no time. . . .

The Lizalfos charged at him once more, his sword raised. Thinking quickly, Link plucked a Bomb Flower that was growing in the chamber and tossed it.

The Lizalfos quickly dodged it, but the explosion created a moment of smoke and confusion. Link took the opportunity to grab his Fairy Slingshot and a Deku Nut from his pack. As soon as the Lizalfos was visible, he let fly a Deku Nut.

The nut hit the Lizalfos's armored chest with a smack, exploding in a flash of bright light. The light had a strange effect on the Lizalfos and it froze for a moment. And a moment was all Link needed. He drew his sword and, ignoring the pain in his leg, lunged at the Lizalfos. He struck before the Lizalfos could attack again.

Panting and in pain, Link climbed up the ladder again. Once he got to the top, he stopped, exhausted.

"Link, you must attend to your leg," Navi warned.

Link nodded, grateful he had bought the potion in the marketplace. He'd have to thank those birds in the Lost Woods.

Link took the bottle of green liquid from his pack. He uncorked the bottle, then raised it to his lips. . . .

Whack! Something flew past Link's face, knocking the bottle out of his hands. Link watched helplessly as the bottle fell to the stone floor and the green liquid spilled out. . . .

He looked around. What had just happened? Then he noticed two Keese hovering on the chamber ceiling, flapping their batlike wings. Link grabbed another Deku Nut and loaded his slingshot. Navi took cover behind Link.

Ping! He hit one of the Keese, knocking it to the floor.

As Link reached for another Deku Nut, the other Keese flew in angry circles around the room. The creature flew right into a torch, which set its body alight with a red glow. It had transformed into a Fire Keese!

Link reached for his Hylian Shield but found he no longer carried it.

I must have lost it when I fell down the ladder, Link realized. He grabbed his Deku Shield, but he knew the wood wouldn't do much good against the Keese's fire attack.

Whoosh! Flames erupted from the Fire Keese, scorching the Deku Shield. The heat burned Link's face, making him suddenly dizzy.

Link jumped up and threw down the shield. He'd have to take down the Keese fast. He aimed the Deku Nut.

Bam! Link hit the Fire Keese just as it readied another attack. Flushed and light-headed, Link sank to the floor.

The pain in his leg was worse now, and with his potion gone, he had no idea how to heal it. He wasn't even sure if he could stand. He lowered his head, exhausted and defeated.

"I'm sorry, Princess," Link whispered. "I have failed you."

A Tie to the Princess

In Hyrule Castle, Princess Zelda walked through the lush gardens. Her mind had been troubled lately with nightmares of the evil that threatened her kingdom. She knew that Link was Hyrule's only hope, and her thoughts never strayed far from him. She felt a special connection with the boy from the forest.

Impa, Zelda's protector, walked a few paces behind the princess everywhere she went. The tall Sheikah was a stern figure with her short hair, muscled limbs, and armored costume, but she had a soft spot when it came to her charge.

Zelda bent down to sniff a white rose. The faint, sweet scent normally filled her with calm. But instead, she jumped back, a look of terror in her eyes.

"Princess, what is it?" Impa asked.

"It's Link," Zelda said. "Something is wrong. Very wrong. I can feel it."

Impa looked over the castle walls, her eyes clouding with concern. "This land is changing," she said. "There are dangers at every turn."

Zelda closed her eyes and tried to concentrate on Link. If she tried hard enough, she could sense him, feel what he was feeling, even see what he was seeing. . . .

Pain. Darkness. Hopelessness. Zelda gasped as the emotions flowed over her. But through it all, a small light shined.

Perhaps things weren't so hopeless after all.

Zelda began to sing her lullaby. Her sweet voice carried over the gardens.

Hear me, Link, Zelda pleaded silently. *Hear my song. . . .*

A Hidden Help

Back in Dodongo's Cavern, Navi landed softly on Link's shoulder.

"I'll go for help," she said. "Don't worry, Link."

The voice of the fairy sounded faint in Link's ear. He felt sleepy, like his body was going numb.

And then he heard Zelda's Lullaby, sung in her own voice. It seemed to drift through the cavern.

"Do you hear that, Navi?" Link asked. "It's the princess."

Navi blinked nervously. "I didn't hear anything, Link. Are you sure?"

Link closed his eyes. Was he sure? The sound of the princess's voice danced through his mind. He took the ocarina from his pack. His breath was weak, but he felt compelled to play the tune.

As Link played, a soft, glowing light filled the chamber. One of the stone walls began to tremble. To Link's amazement, the wall began to shift to the side.

A bright blue light streamed from behind the wall. Link lowered the ocarina and shaded his eyes. He could make out a figure in the light. It was a fairy!

Unlike Navi, this fairy was taller than Link. It was difficult to make out details in the blue glow, but he saw a light blue gown and a beautiful face with blue eyes.

The fairy said nothing, but she didn't have to. Link felt the blue light washing over him. It was stronger than any fairy healing energy he had felt before. The pain in his leg and the throbbing in his head all washed away with the light. Link closed his eyes and drank in the healing.

Soon he heard the door sliding closed. He opened his eyes just in time to see the fairy disappear.

"Thank you," he whispered.

Link jumped to his feet.

"How do you feel?" Navi asked.

"I feel great!" Link cried. Playing Zelda's Lullaby had revealed the hidden chamber, saving him. He wasn't sure exactly what had possessed him to play it, but he had a suspicion. His special connection to Zelda had come to his aid once again.

"Let's find that song and get out of here," Link said. "We've just got to reach one more chamber."

Link cautiously walked through the next doorway, his sword drawn. There were no Lizalfos, no Keese, no other dangerous creatures. But there was no song, either.

Link frowned. "I don't hear anything," he said.

"Listen!" Navi told him.

Link slowed his breathing, trying to hear some kind of sound. At first he couldn't hear anything. But then a faint melody reached his ears.

Five notes repeated over and over, just like the other songs. But where was the sound coming from? Link scanned the chamber, which was empty except for a clump of Bomb Flowers and a puddle of bubbling lava.

The lava ... Link stepped closer. He could see that the bubbles in the pool popped up with precise timing. Each time a bubble burst, it released a *plink!* sound in perfect pitch. Link took out the map and saw the fourth musical note glowing.

"This is it!" Link told Navi. "It's the fourth part of the song."

Link held the Fairy Ocarina to his lips once more and played the tune a few times.

"Just one more to go," Navi remarked when he had finished.

"One more," Link agreed as he looked at the map. "We need to go to Zora's River!"

Link and Navi headed out of the cavern

the same way they had come in. When they reached the spot where Link had fought the Lizalfos, he found the Hylian Shield. Now Link was prepared for anything.

Five Friendly Frogs

The sun shone brightly over Hyrule as Link walked along the banks of Zora's River with Navi flying by his side. The map showed that the last part of the song could be found near the waterfall that led to Zora's Domain. He had quite a way to go.

The fairy healing had left him revitalized once again, and he had eaten some bread and cheese left over from the marketplace. With the Hylian Shield once again slung over his back, he felt more confident about what lay ahead. The bubbling blue waters of Zora's River were a lot nicer than the dank caverns of Death Mountain. Link knelt down and drank deeply from the cool water. It tasted delicious.

Link wiped his mouth with the sleeve of his tunic. The Zoras, a race of fishlike people, guarded the waters of Hyrule, keeping them clean and pure. Link was grateful that the evil threatening the land had not yet reached them.

It was late afternoon by the time Link reached the waterfall that hid the home of the Zoras. Link sat on a rock and listened. The waterfall made a soothing sound as the water hit the river, but it didn't sound like the notes of a tune. The last part of the song was supposed to be here, so why couldn't Link hear it?

"Ribbit ribbit."

A familiar sound reached Link's ears, but it wasn't part of the tune. He looked into the river to see five brightly colored frogs sitting on a mossy log near the river-bank. Each frog was a different color: orange, pink, purple, aqua, and indigo.

"Hello, Link," the frogs croaked in chorus. "Do you have a song for us?"

Link smiled. He had encountered the frogs before. They loved to hear music, especially music Link played on his ocarina.

"I do have a new song," Link said. "But it's not finished yet."

Link took out the Fairy Ocarina and played the four parts of the tune he had learned so far.

The notes floated across the river, joining together to form an eerie yet beautiful tune. The frogs croaked happily when Link finished.

"We have heard that song before," the frogs said. "But when you play it, it is most beautiful."

"Thank you," Link replied. "But I don't know the ending yet."

"We do," the frogs said.

"You do?" Link asked. So the map was right after all!

"Yes," the frogs answered. "Listen."

Link listened to their song and then repeated it on his ocarina. When he took out the map, he saw the last musical note glowing on the page. Navi happily flapped her wings.

"Link! You've done it!" she cried. "We can go close the portal now!"

Link walked down to the river's edge to thank the frogs. "You've helped me more than you will know," he told them.

"You're welcome," the frogs croaked in reply.

Link started to put the ocarina back in his pack. Without warning, a round rock flew out of the river! It smacked into the ocarina, causing Link to lose his grip. He watched helplessly as the ocarina flew across the river, then sank into the water.

Without the ocarina, Link would not be able to close the portal or play Zelda's Lullaby if he was in trouble. He could not let it go. He swiftly stripped himself of his pack and weapons. Then he dove into the water.

"Be careful, Link!" Navi called after him.

Link could see the little flute sinking into the deep water in front of him. He reached out to grab it — and a sticky purple tentacle wrapped around his arm and pulled him underwater!

The Octorok

Link struggled to free himself from the tentacle. The face of a deadly Octorok glared at him with green eyes.

Now I know where that rock came from, Link realized. Octoroks had long, tube-shaped mouths, and they shot rocks from them like weapons.

Link managed to shake off the tentacle. His lungs felt like they would burst. He swam to the top of the water and gasped for air.

The Octorok grabbed his leg, but this

time Link was ready. He reached for his sword. . . .

It wasn't there. Link cringed as he remembered he had left his weapons on the riverbank. The Octorok dragged him down into the water again.

Link kicked violently, but the Octorok's grasp was tight. The purple creature had eight tentacles, each of them equally strong.

Angry, Link kicked harder. The tentacle unfurled, and Link swam to the top of the river. When he reached the surface, he gasped for breath.

He had to swim to the bank to reach his weapons. It was his only hope. He turned toward the shore, but the Octorok grabbed his ankle. Link groaned. With each attack from the Octorok, he felt weaker.

"Link! Look up!" Navi cried.

As the Octorok pulled him under, Link looked up to see his sword dropping down from the sky. He reached and grabbed just before he was pulled under.

Finally, a fair fight, Link told himself. He attacked the Octorok with one quick motion. The tentacle released its grip, and the frightened Octorok swam away.

Link swam to the surface again. Where had the sword come from? Navi was too small to carry it. And then he saw the brown bird circling overhead.

"Hello, Link," said Kaepora Gaebora. "I thought you might need some help. Would you like a ride?"

"One minute," Link replied. "I need to get something."

Link dove back under the water. The

ocarina rested on a rock on the bottom of the river. He swam down and retrieved it. Then he swam back to shore.

The warm sun felt good on his wet body. He wrung out his tunic, and Kaepora Gaebora settled on a tree branch next to him.

"Navi tells me you have found all the parts of the song," the owl said.

Link nodded. "I can close the portal now."

"There is no time to waste," said Kaepora Gaebora. "The portal is growing stronger."

Link put his pack and weapons back on. "How about that ride, then?" he asked.

"Certainly," the owl said. "Just grab on to my talons."

Navi hopped on Link's shoulder as Link grabbed the owl's strong talons. Link nodded good-bye to the frogs as Kaepora Gaebora flew away.

"*Ribbit! Ribbit!*" they croaked together in farewell.

The owl flew swiftly over Hyrule, and the warm breeze quickly dried out Link's wet hair and tunic.

When the owl landed in the center of Kakariko Village, Link saw that the villagers were fleeing their homes.

"Leave this place!" an old man said to him.

"There is an evil in the woods!" said a young girl.

So the owl was right. The vortex was growing stronger.

"Be careful, Link," Navi said. "You almost got sucked in last time."

"That's because I approached the portal

head-on," Link reminded her. "If we approach from the side, we should be fine."

The villagers watched, amazed, as Link bravely headed into the woods. Soon he felt the portal's pull. The sound of the rushing winds of the vortex blanketed the forest.

Link stepped closer, cautiously and slowly. Navi flew just behind his head. Kaepora Gaebora flew above them, going from branch to branch. When the stone wall came into view, Link made sure to stay out of the portal's direct pull. When he was a few feet away, he took out the ocarina.

"Time to close the door," he said as he began playing the notes he had learned on his journey.

As the first notes sounded, the pull from

the vortex grew suddenly stronger. The unexpected surge in power caught Link off guard. He felt the pull lift him off his feet.

"Link!" Navi cried.

Inside the Vortex

The ocarina fell to the ground. Link tried to resist, but the vortex pulled him inside the portal. It felt like a million strong hands had control of his body. He grabbed the edge of the portal, but the pull was too powerful this time. He gasped as the vortex sucked him inside.

"Nooooooo!" Link yelled with all his might. His whole body was inside the portal now, but with one last attempt, he managed to grip a small part of the wall with both hands.

The swirling winds of the vortex roared around his body; inside the wind, he could hear cries of fear and despair. The unearthly cold began to creep over his body, freezing his feet, then his legs. . . .

He had to hold on. He could not give up. Princess Zelda was counting on him. He had to return to Hyrule.

I will not fail you, Princess! Link swore silently as the cold crept closer to his face and hands. Once the evil chill reached his fingers, he knew he would not be able to hang on any longer.

"Link! Hang on!"

A strong, familiar voice echoed in his head. Suddenly, a strong hand gripped his.

The hands heaved mightily, jerking the first half of Link's body out of the vortex.

He took mighty gulps of the clean, warm air.

Impa, Zelda's guard, now gripped both of Link's hands. Zelda nodded at Link as Impa gave another mighty pull.

Link flew out of the portal, knocking Impa to the ground. It was then that Link noticed the strong rope tied around Impa's waist.

"Link! The ocarina," Zelda called.

As the warmth returned to Link's body, his mind felt clearer. He spotted the ocarina within reach on the ground. Impa secured her arms around Link's waist, and with his hands free, Link was able to grab the ocarina.

Link knew just what to do. He put the ocarina to his lips and played the song.

The pull grew stronger again, but Link played on.

Then, something different happened. The more Link played, the weaker the pull of the vortex became. The sound of the roaring winds became fainter and fainter.

With the last five notes, the swirling winds stopped. The hole in the wall closed, and an eerie quiet descended over the woods.

Exhausted, Link put down the ocarina. He rose to his feet.

"Thank you, Impa," he said. "But how did you . . ."

Princess Zelda smiled at Link.

"You are too important to Hyrule, Link," she said. "We couldn't lose you to another dimension."

"Thank you," Link said, looking down at his boots. He always felt slightly awed in the presence of the princess.

Navi flew down and fluttered near his face as Kaepora Gaebora perched on a tree branch next to Link. Impa untied the rope from around her waist. The other end was tied around a thick tree.

"I owe thanks to all of you," Link said. "If you hadn't helped . . ." Link shuddered. He'd probably be at the bottom of Zora's River, or trapped inside the mysterious dimension behind the portal.

"Your mission is our mission, Link," Impa said gravely. "We are sworn to protect Hyrule."

Link looked around the woods. Through the tops of the trees, he could see the sun shining in the bright blue sky. A stray cucco walked past them, clucking and bobbing its head. Link smiled. Hyrule was his home. It was a good home — a place worth saving.

"We will protect Hyrule," Link said. "Together."

Princess Zelda smiled. "Together."

Then the friends left the woods, ready to face the next challenge that crossed their path.